Karen's Two Families

Look for these
and other books about Karen
in the
Baby-sitters Little Sister series:

BABY-SITTERS
Little Sister

Karen's Two Families
Ann M. Martin

Illustrations by Susan Tang

A
LITTLE APPLE
PAPERBACK

SCHOLASTIC INC.
New York Toronto London Auckland Sydney

The author wishes to thank
John C. Esposito, attorney-at-law,
for his suggestions and comments
while preparing this manuscript.

ISBN 0-590-47046-9

12 11 10 9 8 7 6 5 4 3 2 1   4 5 6 7 8 9/9

Printed in the U.S.A.   40

First Scholastic printing, April 1994

Karen's Two Families

Astrid of Grenville

" 'Bye, Daddy!" I called. "I'm going to Maria's house!"

I closed the door behind me. I ran across the lawn to the street. Spring had finally arrived, and I was glad. All winter the grass had been brown and dull-looking. Now it was green again. And thick. It felt like a carpet under my feet. It made me think of a silly poem Mommy had taught me:

Spring has sprung. The grass is green.
I wonder where the flowers been.

(You have to say "been" like "bean.")

Spring has sprung. The grass is ris.
I wonder where the birdies is.

Pretty silly. Andrew loves that poem. (Andrew is my little brother. He is four going on five.)

I looked both ways. Then I crossed the street. I did not go to Maria's house. Not yet. First I went to Hannie's. Hannie Papadakis is one of my best friends. She lives next door to Maria Kilbourne.

I rang Hannie's bell.

"Coming!" called Hannie.

A few moments later Hannie dashed outside. "Okay, let's go!" she cried. She grabbed my hand.

Hannie and I ran to Maria's, and Maria let us inside.

"Where is she? Where is Astrid?" I asked.

"On the sun porch," Maria replied. "Resting."

2

"Resting?" I whispered. "Okay."

My friends and I tiptoed to the sun porch. We peered in at Astrid of Grenville.

"When are the babies due?" I asked.

"Soon," replied Maria. "I do not know how many days. But soon."

Astrid of Grenville is a Bernese mountain dog. She is expecting puppies. Hannie and Maria and I cannot wait. Astrid has had puppies before so we know this will be exciting. Guess what. My stepbrother David Michael has a puppy from Astrid's last litter. He named the puppy Shannon after Maria's big sister!

We sat gently on the couch where Astrid was napping.

"Oh, how are we ever going to be able to wait for the puppies to be born?" I said. "I wish Astrid would have them right now. How many babies do you think she will have, Maria?"

Maria frowned. "I am not sure. But a lot. Maybe eight or ten."

"Wow!" I exclaimed. I paused. "Hey, maybe Mommy or Daddy will let me have a puppy."

Hannie and Maria spoke at exactly the same time. Hannie said, "Karen, you know what your parents said about pets." And Maria said, "Astrid's babies are going to be purebred. We are going to sell them. The puppies will cost a fortune. Plus, a whole bunch of people have already said they want to buy puppies after they are born."

Boo and bullfrogs. Oh, well. I did not *really* think I could have a puppy. We have enough pets already. That was why Mommy and Daddy had said no more. At least, no more big pets.

I sighed. "I know I cannot have a puppy," I said. "I just want to watch Astrid's puppies grow. Maybe I could even watch them be born. That would be cool."

"Well, maybe you could watch," said Maria thoughtfully. "If the puppies are born during the daytime."

"And if you are at your father's house," added Hannie.

Those were some big ifs. But I had a good feeling about Astrid and her puppies. And I was going to think positively. More than anything, I wanted to see those puppies grow.

Missing Daddy

I knew there was a good chance I would *not* be at Daddy's house when Astrid's puppies were born. I would be at Mommy's. You see, I live at two houses. I have two homes. I am a two-two.

Hello. My name is Karen Brewer. I am seven years old. My hair is long, I have some freckles, and my eyes are blue. Some people call me Four-eyes. That is because I wear glasses. I have two pairs. The blue pair is for reading. The pink pair is for the rest of the time.

I am in second grade. I go to a school called Stoneybrook Academy. It is in Stoneybrook, Connecticut, which is where I live. My teacher is Ms. Colman. She is gigundoly nice, the best teacher I have ever had. She never yells. She hardly even gets mad. When I am noisy, and she wants me to settle down, she just says, "Indoor voice, please, Karen."

How did I get two families? Well, I did not always have them. When I was very little, I had just one family: Mommy, Daddy, Andrew, me. We lived together in Daddy's big house. It is the house he grew up in. But after awhile, Mommy and Daddy began to fight. They fought a lot. About everything. Finally they decided they could not live together anymore. They loved Andrew and me very much, but they did not love each other. They were going to get a divorce.

After the divorce, Mommy moved into a little house. It is not *too* far from Daddy's.

Now Andrew and I live at the big house with Daddy every other weekend and on some vacations and holidays. We live at the little house with Mommy the rest of the time. (That is why I would probably be at Mommy's when Astrid's puppies were born.)

Mommy and Daddy have gotten married again (but not to each other). Mommy married a man named Seth. He is my stepfather. Daddy married a woman named Elizabeth. She is my stepmother. And that is how I wound up with two families.

These are the people in my little-house family: Mommy, Seth, Andrew, me. These are the pets: Rocky, Midgie, and Emily Junior. Rocky and Midgie are Seth's cat and dog. Emily Junior is my rat.

These are the people in my big-house family: Daddy, Elizabeth, Andrew, me, Kristy, Charlie, Sam, David Michael, Emily Michelle, and Nannie. Kristy, Charlie, Sam, and David Michael are Elizabeth's kids.

(She was married once before she married Daddy.) So they are my stepsister and stepbrothers. Kristy is thirteen. I just love her. She is a good baby-sitter. Charlie and Sam are old. They go to high school. David Michael is seven like me. But he does not go to my school. Emily Michelle is my adopted sister. Daddy and Elizabeth adopted her from the faraway country of Vietnam. She is two and a half. I named my rat after her. Nannie is Elizabeth's mother, which makes her my stepgrandmother. She helps take care of the house and us kids, since Daddy and Elizabeth both work.

The pets at the big house are Boo-Boo, Shannon, Goldfishie, and Crystal Light the Second. Boo-Boo is Daddy's fat old cat, Shannon is the puppy I told you about, and Goldfishie and Crystal Light are (what else?) goldfish!

Remember when I said I am a two-two? I am Karen Two-Two because I have two of so many things. I have two homes and two families, two mommies and two daddies, two cats and two dogs. Andrew is a two-two, too. I used to think we were lucky. But lately I have been changing my mind.

David Michael's Play

Not everyone can have two of all the things I have. Do you know what? I even have two best friends. Hannie is my big-house best friend. She lives across the street from Daddy and one house down. Nancy Dawes is my little-house best friend. She lives next door to Mommy.

Having two best friends is nice, but there are some things I wish I did not have to have two of. For instance, I have two stuffed cats that look exactly alike. Moosie stays at the big house, Goosie stays at the

12

little house. And I have two pieces of Tickly, my special blanket. But do you know *why*? It is so I will not have to remember to bring them with me when I go from house to house. Before — when I had only one Tickly — I used to leave him behind at one place or the other, and then I would cry and carry on, and someone would have to go get him for me. Finally I tore Tickly in two.

You see, there are some problems with being a two-two. For Andrew and me, the biggest problem is we only get to see Daddy and our big-house family two weekends each month. That is only four *days* each month. Nothing. We miss Daddy a lot.

The day that Hannie and I visited Astrid of Grenville was a Saturday. It was the Saturday of a big-house weekend. When I finished petting Astrid and talking to my friends, I ran back to Daddy's. I love big-house weekends, and I did not want to miss a thing. Plus, this seemed to be an extra busy weekend.

13

Guess what. The weekend was so busy that by the time I was at home again, hardly anyone else was there. Only Daddy and Andrew.

"Where is everybody?" I asked.

"Let me see," replied Daddy. "Kristy is over at Bart's house, Nannie is in a bowling tournament, Charlie and Sam are watching baseball tryouts at school, and Elizabeth and Emily took David Michael to school for a rehearsal."

"Rehearsal? What rehearsal?" I asked.

"David Michael is in *The Wizard of Oz,*" said Daddy. "He plays one of the Winkies. Today he will get his costume."

"He is in *The Wizard of Oz?*" I repeated. "I did not know that. When did that happen? Boy, I miss everything around here."

Just then Daddy looked at his watch. "Uh-oh," he said.

"What?" I asked.

"I just remembered. I have a tennis game in an hour."

"To*day?*" I cried. "But Daddy . . ."

14

"I'm sorry," said Daddy. "I guess I forgot you two were going to be here this weekend. I got my dates confused."

Andrew looked as if he were going to cry. I wanted to cry, too. But then Daddy said, "Oh, well. It is just a tennis game. I will cancel it. I can play tennis any time. But I hardly ever see you guys."

I knew how Daddy felt. Phew! I was glad he canceled his game.

Daddy and Andrew and I read stories together. We read until Elizabeth came home with Emily Michelle and David Michael. As soon as I saw them, I jumped to my feet. "Hey, David Michael! Can I try on your Winkie costume?" I asked him.

"Sure," he replied.

"Boy. I cannot believe I didn't know about your play."

"I guess you were not here when I tried out for it."

"I am hardly *ever* here," I replied grumpily.

Big Enough

My grumpy mood did not last long. The rest of the weekend was too much fun. When everyone in my big-house family had finally come home, Daddy said, "Well, it is a little early in the season, but let's have a barbecue. Then we can have an indoor picnic."

So we did.

On Sunday, Kristy and I took a bicycle ride. After that, Nannie let me go with her to bowling practice. When it was time to return to the little house, I did not want to leave. I cried while Daddy drove us to Mommy's.

Mommy met Andrew and me at the front door. "Karen? What is the matter?" she asked.

"I did not want to come back," I mumbled. "I was not ready to leave the big house yet. Two days there is too short."

I flumped up to my room. I let Emily Junior out of her cage, and I held her in my lap for awhile. I could hear Andrew grumbling around in his room. He was not happy either. At the big house, he and Sam were making a model airplane. Andrew would have to wait two weeks before they could paint bat eyes on the wings.

After awhile, Andrew stuck his head in my room. He glared at me. "I wanted to finish that plane, Karen," he said.

"I know you did. You are mad. So am I."

Andrew pointed to Emily Junior. "Well, at least you have a pet of your own. I do not even have a pet."

"You do too. Goldfishie is your very own goldfish," I reminded him.

"Oh, Goldfishie does not count. He has to stay at the big house. I hardly ever see him. David Michael takes care of him."

"Well, what about Midgie and Rocky?" I asked my brother. "They live here."

Andrew made a face at me. "They are not *mine!*" he exclaimed, as if I should have known better. "They are Seth's. I want my own pet. And I want to take care of it all by myself."

"So I guess helping me take care of Emily Junior would not be good enough."

"No way," said Andrew.

"Then you better talk to Mommy and Seth," I told him.

Andrew did not wait very long. At supper that night he said, "Excuse me. Excuse me, everybody."

"Yes, Andrew?" said Seth.

"I have to say something very important. I would like to have a pet of my own. I am big enough. I would take good care of it."

18

"Well . . ." Mommy began.

"Karen has a pet of her own — at *each* house. And David Michael has a pet. But all the other pets belong to grown-ups."

I looked at Mommy. Mommy was looking at Seth.

"Please?" said Andrew.

"We'll see," replied Mommy.

When supper was over Andrew came into my room again. "Do you think Mommy will let me get a pet?" he asked.

I was not sure. Mommy had said, "We'll see." That could mean anything. I did not want to disappoint Andrew. But I did not want to get his hopes up, either. Just in case. So I said, "You know what? I really do not know. But I have a suggestion. Do not bug Mommy about the pet, okay? Do not bug Seth, either. Let it alone for awhile and just see what happens."

"Okay," replied Andrew. He looked more cheerful. "I am going to go dream about the perfect pet now."

Emily's Bed

Mommy did not say anything more about a pet. I reminded Andrew not to ask her about it. "Do not be a pest," I said. "Not if you want Mommy and Seth to think you are old enough for a pet."

I gave Andrew something else to think about instead. We began a countdown until the day we could go back to the big house. We shouted out the numbers every morning when we woke up. "Five more days!" Then, "Four more days!" And finally, "One more day!" And best of all, "Today! Today is the day!"

Seth drove us to the big house in time for supper on Friday. "Good-bye!" we called to him. "See you on Sunday!"

Then we ran to the front door.

"I wonder if everyone will be here," said Andrew.

"Maybe not. So do not be upset," I warned him.

But guess what. Before I could put my hand on the knob, the door flew open. There was David Michael in his Winkie costume. There was Kristy. There was Emily. There was my entire big-house family.

I needed a long time to hug everybody.

"What is for dinner?" asked Andrew when the hugging was over.

"Lasagna," said Elizabeth. "We are going to have an Italian meal tonight. Lasagna and garlic bread and salad."

"And we will speak Italian," I added.

"Do you know any Italian?" Daddy asked.

"Sure," I replied. "Fribber barber moo-goo blinky."

Daddy laughed. "Okay, let's eat."

We sat at the table in the kitchen. We can just barely fit at it, even though it is long. Four people on one side, four on the other, Nannie (or one of the grown-ups) at one end, Emily in her high chair at the other end. When we had been served our Italian meal, we began to talk. (We spoke in English.)

"Tess and I are writing a report together," said Kristy.

"Who is Tess?" I asked.

"My new friend. You met her, didn't you, Karen? She came over last — Oh, I guess you were not here. Well, anyway, you will like her."

Then Nannie said that her bowling team was going to be in the play-offs, starting the next day.

"The play-offs?" I repeated. "You made the play-offs? The last time I was here you

did not think you would make the semi-finals."

"Oh, well, that was two weeks ago. Anyway, do you want to come to our big game tomorrow?"

"Sure!" I replied.

Nannie's game was going to be on Saturday afternoon. On Saturday morning I was playing on our driveway with Kristy and Emily when a truck pulled in. The sign on the side said TUCKER FURNITURE.

"Hey! What are we getting?" I asked.

"I'm not sure," Kristy replied.

We watched as two movers unloaded an enormous box.

"Oh, I bet I know what that is!" exclaimed Kristy. "I just remembered. It must be Emily's new big-girl bed. Look, Emily!"

"Her what? Why didn't I know about that?" I cried. When had Emily gotten big enough for a big-girl bed? That was very important. It meant Emily Michelle was growing up.

I just could not believe all the things Andrew and I missed out on while we were at the little house. It was double not fair. NOT NOT FAIR FAIR.

Boo and bullfrogs.

Astrid's Puppies

On Saturday afternoon, I went to the bowling alley with Nannie. Her team won their big game. They were very excited.

On Sunday, Andrew and I went back to the little house.

On Monday, I went back to school.

On Tuesday, Hannie had big news.

It was early in the morning. Nancy and I were already at school. We were sitting on two desks in the back of our classroom. Ms. Colman had not arrived yet, and neither had most of the kids.

Suddenly Hannie burst into the room. "Karen! Nancy! I am glad you are here," she cried. "Guess what. Astrid had her puppies last night!"

"Oh, she did? Cool!" exclaimed Nancy. "How many did she have?"

"Eight," said Hannie. "I already saw them. Maria called me really early this morning. She said to come right over, so I did."

"Ooh. What did they look like?" asked Nancy.

"All squirmy."

"Are they cute?"

"Well . . . not yet. But they will be."

Nancy turned to me. "Isn't this exciting, Karen?"

I was trying to be excited. Honest. But all I could say was, "Darn! I wanted to see the puppies, too. Now I will not be back at the big house for ten more days. The puppies will be ancient by then."

"Karen. They will not," said Hannie.

I pouted. "Well, they will not be newborns. I wanted to see newborn puppies. And now I can't. I hate being a two-two!"

"You do not have to wait ten days to see the puppies," Hannie told me. "Come over to my house. Come any afternoon. Then we can visit the puppies together."

But I knew I wouldn't be able to go that afternoon, or Wednesday afternoon, or Thursday afternoon. (I would have to see about Friday.) I was busy with little-house things. Boo and bullfrogs.

I noticed that Nancy was frowning at me. "What do you mean you hate being a two-two?" she asked. "I thought you liked it."

"I used to," I admitted. "But lately I feel like I miss out on *every*thing at the big house. I did not know Emily was big enough for a big-girl bed. I did not know about Nannie's bowling team. I do not even know Kristy's friends now. Plus, I miss Daddy all the time. I miss everyone. The pets, too. I am only at the big house four days each month, you know. That is not much time at all. It is hardly anything."

"Boy," said Hannie. "I used to wish I could be a two-two like you."

I sighed. "I guess it is not *all* bad," I said after awhile. "Having two families can be fun. I get lots of vacations, because I go on vacations with my little-house family and then I go on vacations with my big-house family. And having two houses is fun, too. I like my room at the little house because it is new. Mommy let me choose the furniture for it myself. And I like my room at the big house because it is old. It is the room I grew up in. Not everybody can have a new *and* an old bedroom." I paused. "But nothing makes up for missing Daddy and not knowing the important things that are happening to the people at the big house. Not even having two birthday parties each year. I wish I were not a two-two."

"Karen, I do not think that will change," said Nancy.

"I know. But I wish it could."

I was very quiet that day. I felt a little sad.

Yipes!

Just as I had thought, I could not go to Hannie's house that Tuesday afternoon. And I could not go on Wednesday or Thursday. But on Friday morning, I said to Mommy, "Could I go to Hannie's after school today? I do not have any plans."

Mommy looked at her calendar. "Fine with me," she said.

"Yes!" I cried. I would be able to see Astrid's puppies when they were only four days old. That was still *pretty* little. Not newborn, but better than waiting until they were ten days old.

Mrs. Papadakis drove Hannie and me home after school. In the car, I was so excited about the puppies that I could not sit still. I kept bouncing around.

"I am glad you are wearing a seatbelt, Karen," said Mrs. Papadakis. "Otherwise you might bounce right out of the window."

When Mrs. Papadakis pulled into the driveway, Hannie and I zipped out of the car. We ran right next door to Maria's. We raced to see who could reach the doorbell first. I won. But I let Hannie ring the bell.

"Hi!" cried Maria when she opened the door. "Hi, you guys! Karen, I am glad you could visit the puppies. They are so cute."

Maria led us to Astrid's box. I sat on the floor. I peered inside. "Hi, Astrid," I whispered.

Astrid was lying on her side. The puppies were wriggling against her tummy. They were mashed together in a pile.

"They *are* squirmy!" I cried softly.

They were tiny, too. Little fat bodies with short legs and big heads. They did not look much like dogs. They looked more like hamsters.

"Are they asleep?" I asked Maria. "They are eating, but their eyes are closed. They do not look like they are asleep."

"Their eyes have not opened," Maria replied. "They will not open for awhile. The puppies do everything with their eyes closed."

"How do you know if they are awake or asleep?" I asked.

Maria shrugged.

I watched the puppies for awhile. They seemed to be awfully hungry. They kept nursing from Astrid. Astrid was patient. She nosed the puppies around so they all had a chance to eat. She licked them to keep them clean. And she made sure the puppies did not get squished or move too far away from her.

"Aren't they sweet?" asked Hannie.

"Adorable," I replied.

"You can touch them," Maria said to me. "But only a little. And you cannot pick them up yet. That makes Astrid nervous."

I reached into the box and stroked one of the puppies with my finger. It felt as soft as a whisper of wind.

"You know what?" said Maria after awhile. "People have been calling and calling about the puppies. We have already sold all but one of them. My mom says we will sell the last puppy, too, in no time."

"How much do they cost?" I asked. I thought Maria might say ten dollars each. But when she told me the price, I yelped. "Yipes! That really is a fortune!" The Kilbournes were going to earn thousands of dollars by selling the puppies.

Later, when Hannie and I were leaving Maria's house, I said sadly, "I do not know when I will be able to see the puppies again."

Hannie promised to tell me about them in school every day.

Andrew's Pet

At dinner that night, I told my little-house family about the puppies.

"They are so tiny," I said. "They could sit in your hand. In one hand. Except that you are not allowed to pick them up. And their eyes have not opened yet. Mostly they just sleep and eat."

"Can they walk?" asked Andrew.

I shook my head. "Nope. They squirm around, though."

"I wish I could see them," said Andrew.

"I will take you to Maria's the next time

we are at the big house," I told him. "Oh, guess what. All but one of the puppies has been sold. Maria says the last one will probably be sold soon."

"They have been sold?" repeated Andrew. "Then how can I see them?"

"Oh, they have not gone to their new homes yet. They cannot go until they are much bigger."

Andrew nodded. He looked thoughtful. Then suddenly he grinned. "Hey!" he cried. "Could I have that last puppy? The one that has not been sold? Please? It could be my pet. Puh-*lease*, Mommy?"

Well, for heaven's sake. I had not told Andrew he could ask for a pet yet. I had not said it was time. But he had not been a pest lately, so I guessed it was all right for him to ask Mommy again.

Still, I did not think she would let Andrew have Astrid's last puppy. For one thing, we already had a dog at the little house. We had Midgie. For another thing, Andrew might be old enough to take care

36

of a little goldfish or something, but I was pretty sure he was not old enough to take care of a dog. Also, Astrid's puppy was way too expensive. We could not afford to spend so much money on a pet. We could get a free puppy at the pound.

Sure enough, Mommy said, "A puppy would be a nice pet, Andrew. But we already have a dog. One is enough. Anyway, I do not think you are quite ready to care for a dog."

"Boo," said Andrew. He put his fork down and rested his chin in his hands.

"But," Mommy went on, "Seth and I have been talking about your pet."

"You have?" said Andrew. He sat up straight. He smiled.

"Yes. We have decided you may get a pet of your own — "

"All *right!*" cried Andrew.

" — as long as it is a small pet that is very easy to care for."

"Like a kitten?" Andrew asked hopefully.

"No," replied Seth. "A kitten is small, but it is not easy to care for. We were thinking of a fish or a turtle."

"Hmm," said Andrew. "Hmm. Let me see."

Uh-oh. Andrew had forgotten something very important. There was something he needed to say to Mommy and Seth. I mouthed the words at him from across the table: "Thank you."

"What?" Andrew said to me.

"THANK YOU," I mouthed again.

"You're — " Andrew started to say. Then he stopped. "Oh! Oh, um, thank you, Mommy. Thank you, Seth."

"You're welcome," they replied.

"So what kind of pet are you going to get?" I asked my brother.

Andrew frowned. "I do not know yet. I will have to think about it."

I could tell Andrew was going to take a long time with his decision. He would want to choose exactly the right pet. Maybe he would make up his mind the next day.

Guess what. Andrew did not make up his mind the next day — or the next day or the next. Then on Monday, something happened that made me forget about Andrew's pet.

Whose Rules?

On Monday morning, Hannie walked into our classroom with a grin on her face. She ran to join Nancy and me. "I held one of the puppies!" she announced. "I was at Maria's house yesterday, and her mom said Maria and I could each pick up a puppy. So we did."

"Aww!" said Nancy.

"And the puppy nuzzled me and squirmed around just as if I were Astrid. But then he whimpered, so I put him down right away."

I could not believe Hannie had actually held one of the puppies. I had not seen them since Friday. I had been busy with little-house things, and anyway, no one could drive me over to Hannie's house.

"And then, you know what two of the puppies did?" Hannie said.

"No, what?" asked Nancy.

"They started . . . Karen?" said Hannie. "What is the matter?"

I was pouting and I knew it. But I could not help it. "Well, it is just no fair!" I cried.

"What is no fair?" asked Nancy. She and Hannie looked confused.

"It is no fair that I can only go to Daddy's every other weekend!"

"Just because of the puppies?" asked Hannie, sounding surprised.

"No! Because of the puppies and — and — and *every*thing. By the time I go back there this weekend, the puppies will probably be all grown-up, and Emily Michelle will know how to read, and David Michael

will be a TV star, and Nannie will be a pro bowler."

Hannie and Nancy and I looked at each other. Nancy began to giggle. I almost giggled too, but then I said, "I really do miss my big-house family, you know. I feel like I am not part of them. Andrew feels the same way. We have talked about it." I sighed. "I hate the custody arrangements. I hate the rules about where Andrew and I have to go, and when, and for how long."

"Well, who made up those rules?" someone asked.

I had not realized how loudly I had been talking. Now I saw that Ricky Torres was standing nearby. He had heard everything I had said. (I did not mind. Ricky is my friend. In fact, he is my pretend husband. We got married on the playground one day.)

"Who made up those rules?" I repeated. "I don't know. I guess Mommy and Daddy and their lawyers did."

"Can't you change them?" asked Ricky.

"Well . . . I don't know," I said again. "Mommy and Daddy have told me the arrangements are really hard to change. You can't just change them like you change out of clothes you don't like. Plus, what if we did change them and I did not like the *new* arrangements?"

"Well, anyway," Ricky went on, "my aunt and uncle got divorced, and my cousins have equal time with them. They spend a week with their mom, then a week with their dad."

"Cool!" I exclaimed.

Somebody else had been listening to us. "I have a friend," said Pamela Harding, "whose parents are divorced, too." (Pamela Harding is my best enemy, but just then I did not care. I wanted to hear about her friend.) "My friend spends a *year* with her mom, then a *year* with her dad. Her parents live far apart," added Pamela.

"A *year*," I repeated. "Boy, what a long time."

"But it is equal time," Ricky pointed out.

"Yeah, equal time," I agreed. "Not four days a month at one house and twenty-six or twenty-seven days at the other house."

"That is kooky," said Ricky.

I was not sure it was kooky, but it certainly was not equal. I needed to think about equal time. It was a new idea. More important, I would have to think about changing the rules. *Could* I do that? Could a kid change the rules? I would have to find out.

A Madhouse

I could not stop thinking about equal time with Mommy and Daddy. It seemed so much fairer than twenty-six days with Mommy and four days with Daddy. But I did not know whether I could change that.

While Andrew and I waited for the next big-house weekend, we began another countdown. We were so happy on Friday when we could shout, "Today is the day!" Andrew wanted to paint those bat eyes on his airplane with Sam. I wanted to find out

46

how David Michael was doing in *The Wizard of Oz*. And we both wanted to see Daddy.

On Friday night we had pizza for dinner at the big house. I love pizza. And I love pizza parties. But I guess I was busy thinking about equal time again, because after dinner, Kristy said to me, "Karen? You are very quiet this evening."

"I am?" I replied. (Kristy nodded.) "Usually you are our chatterbox. Is anything wrong?"

"I am just thinking," I told her.

"Do you want to talk about whatever it is?"

"Well . . . maybe. Let me go to my room and decide."

In my room I sat on my bed. I held Tickly in one hand. I hugged Moosie with the other. Did I want to talk to Kristy? Hmm. I should probably talk to someone. And Kristy would be a good person to start with. I trust Kristy. I have told her lots of secrets, and she has kept them all. Plus, Kristy's parents are divorced. Just like Mommy and Daddy. She would probably understand that I wanted equal time.

I ran to Kristy's room. "Okay, I am ready to talk," I announced.

Kristy smiled at me. She patted her bed, so I sat next to her.

"I have been thinking a lot lately," I began. "What I decided is that spending only four days every month at the big house does not seem fair. Andrew and I miss all the good stuff here. I did not know about Emily's big-girl bed, or David Michael's play, or anything. Plus we miss *you*."

"We miss you and Andrew, too," said Kristy.

"In school," I went on, "Ricky told me that his cousins spend equal time with their parents. Pamela Harding knows a girl who does the same thing. I wish Andrew and I could."

"You mean, spend more time here?" asked Kristy.

"Spend *equal* time here," I replied firmly.

"Hmm. I do not know if the lawyers would let you. The court has to decide things like that. I don't think custody arrangements are changed very easily," said Kristy. "Plus, I do not know what your mom and dad would think. Your mom would miss you and Andrew a lot. Just like you miss us a lot now."

"That's true," I said slowly.

"Anyway, the big house is already a madhouse!" teased Kristy. "It is full of people and pets. It is overflowing."

"I know."

"Besides, you are lucky you can see your father at all. I do not even know where my father is. I have not seen him in years."

I sighed. Kristy was not being helpful. But I was not going to give up on my new idea. The next day, when I visited Astrid and her puppies, I stopped at Hannie's house first. I told her what Kristy had said.

Hannie frowned. "Well, Kristy is not *al-*

ways right," she told me. (We both knew that Kristy is usually right, though.) "Why don't you talk to Ms. Colman? She can solve any problem," said Hannie.

Of course! Why hadn't I thought of that myself?

Ms. Colman's Advice

I had to wait until Monday to see Ms. Colman. Then on Monday, I had to wait until lunchtime to talk to her. That was the first quiet moment in our classroom. I stayed behind when the other kids left for the cafeteria.

"Ms. Colman?" I said. I was still sitting at my desk. My desk is right in front of Ms. Colman's. They touch each other.

"Oh! Karen, you are still here. Is something wrong?"

"I need to talk to you," I said. "I have a problem."

Ms. Colman put down her red pencil. "Okay, go ahead."

"It is about Mommy and Daddy," I began. "I mean, it is about spending time with Mommy and Daddy." I told Ms. Colman what I had told Kristy. I told her about Ricky and Pamela, and about missing my big-house family. Finally I said, "Ricky's cousins can spend equal time with their parents. That is what Andrew and I want to do. We have talked about it," I added.

Ms. Colman looked thoughtful. Then she said gently, "Karen, I know this is not what you want to hear me say, but you need to talk to your parents about this. To both of them. And you need to plan ahead of time what you are going to say. Then say it calmly. After that, ask them what they think about the arrangements. That is really all you can do."

Well, boo. Ms. Colman was right. She had not said what I was hoping to hear. I wanted my teacher to take care of my problem for me. But I guess she could not do that.

"Okay. Thank you," I said to Ms. Colman. "I will start thinking and planning right now. This is going to be a big job."

When I arrived home from school that day, I said to Mommy, "I have been thinking very hard about something. It is important. Can we talk about it tonight after dinner? That would be a good time for our appointment. Let's say eight o'clock."

Eight o'clock was fine with Mommy. Next I called Daddy at his office.

"May I make an appointment to talk with you tonight?" I asked him.

"Of course," replied Daddy.

"Good. I will call you at eight-thirty."

When I got off the phone, I thought about the things I planned to say.

Mommy and Daddy

At eight o'clock, Mommy and I sat down in the den. Mommy was very serious about our talk. She made sure Andrew would not disturb us. And she said, "Do you want Seth to join us, or is this just you and me?"

"Just you and me," I replied.

"Okay," said Mommy.

I drew in a deep breath. I reminded myself to stay calm and to act like a grown-up. I was not going to whine or pout or beg. "Mommy," I began, "Andrew and I have not been happy about something lately. We miss Daddy and our big-house family. We want to spend more time with them. We want equal time, please." I told Mommy why. I told her about the big-girl bed and David Michael's play, but mostly about how sad Andrew and I felt sometimes.

When I stopped talking, Mommy took my hand. She held it for a moment, so I knew she was not angry. Even so, she said, "Karen, I do not think the custody arrangements are going to change. They have been working fine for several years now. Besides, I do not want to spend less time with you and Andrew. I would miss you very much if you were not living here."

"But we would still live here," I said. "Just — just not quite as often. And Andrew and I miss Daddy now. We miss him a lot of the time." I almost said, "That is not fair," but I changed my mind. I decided it would sound whiney.

"I know things are not perfect — "
Mommy started to say.

"They do not have to be perfect," I interrupted her. "Just better."

"Karen, this is an adult decision,"
Mommy went on.

I wanted to say, "But it is about the kids."
I kept my mouth closed, though. I was not going to interrupt again.

"A lot of people needed a lot of time to figure out the custody arrangements. And a judge said the arrangements were okay. They were not meant to be changed. And I really do not *want* to change them. And I do not want to see less of you and Andrew," Mommy told me.

I decided not to argue. "All right," I said. I left the room.

A few minutes later I telephoned Daddy. He was waiting for my call. He told me he was in a quiet place where he would not be bothered.

"Good," I said. "Thank you." Then I told

him pretty much what I had told Mommy. I finished by saying, "Andrew and I wish we could have equal time. Please."

I heard Daddy sigh. "Whew," he said. "Honey, I wish we could have equal time, too. I would like nothing better than to see lots more of you and Andrew. You don't know how much I miss you guys."

"Probably as much as we miss you."

"But I do not think your mother would agree to the change."

"Could you talk to her about it?" I asked. I let myself feel a teensy bit hopeful.

"I could, but that would just cause trouble. And I do not want that. Besides, arrangements are arrangements. Lawyers and a judge helped us make this decision. We have to stick to it."

"You mean it cannot be changed?" I cried.

"Nooo. . . . It could. But it is more complicated than that, Karen. And this is not really my decision."

When Daddy and I got off the phone, I went to my room. I lay on my bed and stared at the ceiling. I felt weak. No one would listen to me. Why wouldn't they hear me? I had no voice or power at all.

Ribbons

The weeks were going by. Every single one of the puppies had been sold. They were growing bigger and older. I felt sad a lot of the time, but not when I was around the puppies. They could always make me laugh.

Mommy let me visit the puppies pretty often. Maybe she felt bad because she knew how much I missed being at the big house. She had said no to equal time, and I had not bugged her about it. Just like Andrew had not bugged her for a pet. Bugging her would make me look like a baby. Besides, I had a feeling I could not change her mind. I tried to let things go.

The puppies took my mind off of my troubles. One day, when Hannie and I went to Maria's house, we found a surprise. Several of the puppies wore ribbons around their necks — one blue, one purple, one red.

"Hey!" I cried. "Why are the puppies dressed up?"

"They aren't dressed up," Maria replied. She was smiling. "They are wearing the ribbons so we can tell them apart. The owners are starting to choose the puppies they will take home. The Francos chose the one with the red ribbon. Mr. Evans chose the one with the blue ribbon. And Miss Fallon chose the one with the purple ribbon."

"Oh," I said. The ribbons were a very smart idea.

"Someone else is coming to choose a puppy today," Maria went on. "Want to stay and watch?"

"Sure," said Hannie and I.

A few minutes later the doorbell rang. Maria ran to answer it. Soon she and her mother came back with a man and a woman.

"Girls," said Mrs. Kilbourne, "meet Mr. and Mrs. Dodson."

The Dodsons hurried to the pen and peered in at the puppies. The puppies looked much more like puppies now. Their eyes were open, and they could yip and walk and tumble around. They liked to play, and a few of them had tried to climb out of the pen.

"Aw, isn't that one cute?" said Mrs. Dodson.

"Look at *this* one," said Mr. Dodson. He pointed to a different puppy.

"I like the markings on his face," agreed Mrs. Dodson. "He looks as if he is wearing a mask."

I could hardly tell the puppies apart, but their markings *were* a little different. I watched while the Dodsons chose just the right puppy. (It was the one with the mask.) Mrs. Kilbourne tied a green ribbon around its neck.

"Come back any time you want to visit your puppy," said Mrs. Kilbourne. "I know you will be happy with him."

But would the puppy be happy with the Dodsons?

I nudged Maria. "What do you know about the Dodsons?" I asked her. "Do they have a yard for the puppy to play in? Do they have any kids? Do they live near a busy street?"

"Hmm. I do not know," replied Maria.

Maria and Hannie and I spent the next half hour making a questionnaire. We decided we would copy it and give it to the people who were buying the puppies. Then we would know about the homes the puppies were going to. And we could say things to the buyers like, "Since you live on a busy street, make sure your puppy stays in the backyard." Or, "We notice that you do not have any children. Now, puppies like to play. So make sure you play with the puppy yourself. And give it plenty of exercise."

When the questionnaires were finished, my friends and I were not so worried.

Trouble

Of course, I could not spend all day at Maria's house with the puppies. I could not go there every afternoon, or even every other afternoon. And in between visits, I felt very sad. Not because I could not see the puppies. I felt sad because Mommy and Daddy would not give Andrew and me equal time.

I wished my life were different.

I wished it so much that it was all I could think about. I thought about it in school when I was supposed to be working. I thought about it at night when I was supposed to be sleeping.

"Karen," Ms. Colman said to me in school one day, "where are your math worksheets? The ones with the subtraction facts?"

I shrugged. "I don't know."

"You did not finish them yesterday. You were supposed to take them home with you and finish them last night."

"I was? I'm sorry. I did not remember."

Ms. Colman frowned at me. "That is not like you, Karen."

I shrugged again. "Can I go sit down, please?"

"Okay," replied Ms. Colman with a big sigh.

That afternoon, Ms. Colman called on me during a science discussion. "What do you think, Karen?" she asked.

"About what?" (I had not been listening.)

Ms. Colman let out another sigh. It was even bigger than her sigh that morning. "Please pay attention, Karen."

66

The next day something interesting happened during reading. Audrey Green was reading aloud. We were following along in our books. I felt my eyes begin to close, so I put my head down on my desk. The next thing I knew Ms. Colman was shaking my shoulder. "Karen, Karen. Karen?" she was saying.

I opened my eyes. "What?"

"What time did you go to bed last night?"

"Early. But I could not sleep."

"Karen, this cannot continue. I am going to have to call your mother and talk to her."

"Okay," I replied.

I really did not care what Ms. Colman did.

Lawyers

Ms. Colman did call Mommy. She called her that very afternoon, right after school. I was sitting on the couch in front of the TV. Andrew was with me. A cartoon show was on. Andrew was watching it, but I was not. I was just sitting there. Nancy had invited me over to play, but I did not feel like playing.

When the phone rang, Mommy picked it up in the next room. "Oh, hi!" I heard her say. "What? . . . She fell asleep? Well, I don't — " After a long pause, she said, "I know, I know. Karen has always loved school. That is why I am surprised to hear that her work is slipping." (That was when I knew Ms. Colman was on the other end of the line.) After another pause, I heard Mommy say, "I admit she has seemed sad lately. . . . No, she and Nancy haven't played together much lately. Or she and Hannie, for that matter."

Mommy lowered her voice then, and I could not hear her anymore. I thought about tiptoeing to the kitchen to eavesdrop, but I did not really feel like doing that. I did not care what they were talking about.

After awhile, Mommy came into the room. She clicked off the TV. "Andrew," she said, "I would like to talk to Karen in private for a few minutes. You may watch the TV in my bedroom, if you like."

Andrew pouted. His cartoon had been interrupted. "Oh, all right," he said. He stalked out of the room.

Mommy sat beside me on the couch. "Honey, Ms. Colman just telephoned," she told me. "She is worried about you. She said your work is slipping and you are not paying attention. She said you even fell asleep this morning. And she said you seem sad all the time. You seem sad to Seth and me, too."

"Can I put the cartoons back on?" I asked.

"No. We are going to talk. Karen, why are you sad?" I shrugged. Mommy paused. Then she said, "What would make you feel better?"

"I don't know."

"How about the puppy? Astrid's last puppy? Maybe we could get another dog after all."

"It has been sold. They have all been sold."

"Oh." Mommy drew in her breath. "This is about the custody arrangements, isn't it? That is why you are so sad."

"I guess. . . . I mean, yes. That is why I am sad. Andrew is sad, too, you know. That is why he pouts all the time."

"All right," said Mommy. "I will talk to your father."

Mommy looked at me. I think she expected me to smile or something, but I could not. I was afraid to. I had let myself feel hopeful once before. Then I had been disappointed. I did not want that to happen again. I would wait and see.

I did not have to wait long. Mommy left me. She went back to the kitchen. She called Daddy at work and they talked. Mostly, I did not listen. But before Mommy hung up, I heard her say, "All right. I will call John Sachs. You call Peter." (They are our lawyers.) The next thing I knew, Mommy was saying to Mr. Sachs, "About the custody arrangements, John. . . ."

Mommy was on the phone a lot during the next few days.

Finally I let myself feel just an intsy bit hopeful.

Oops!

I did not ask Mommy or Daddy about the arrangements. I did not ask about the lawyers or the phone calls. Something was going on, and I was feeling hopeful. But I did not want to be disappointed again. So I tried to think about other things.

Of course, I thought about the puppies. Boy, were they different now. Maria and her family let them out of the pen sometimes. They ran around the Kilbournes' rec room. They tussled with each other. They played tug-of-war with their toys. I had forgotten how much fun Shannon had been when she was that little.

"They are perfect puppies," I said to Maria one day.

"Yeah." Maria smiled. "I wish they could stay just this size forever. Not too big and not too small."

Mommy had driven me to Maria's house that day after school. Hannie had been invited, too, but she had a play date with another friend. Maria and I were on the floor in the rec room. We were surrounded by puppies. They yipped and scampered and leaped around us. Maria and I started to giggle and could not stop.

"Play gently, girls!" Mrs. Kilbourne called to us from the other room. "And only ten more minutes. Then the puppies will need to rest."

"Okay!" Maria called back.

I grabbed a rubber ball and rolled it across the room. A herd of puppies chased after it, their ribbons flying.

"Sometimes I wish they didn't have to

wear the ribbons," I said to Maria. "They look like furry birthday presents."

Maria giggled. "I know. But we would *never* be able to tell them apart without the ribbons."

A few minutes later, Mrs. Kilbourne entered the room. She helped us put the puppies back in the pen. Then she shooed us out.

"Boo," I said. "I wanted to stay."

"Well, come up to my room," said Maria. "We can look at the questionnaires. Four people filled them out and gave them back to me."

We ran to Maria's room. We read the answers the owners had written on the papers. I had been worried about things like traffic, or no yard to play in, or living cooped up in a little apartment.

"You know what?" I said to Maria after we had looked at the questionnaires. "I think the puppies are going to good homes. We do not need to worry." I checked my watch then. "Hey!" I exclaimed. "Seth is going to pick me up in ten minutes."

"We better peek at the puppies again then," replied Maria.

"But your mom said to leave them alone."

"She said not to *play* with them. She did not say we could not *look* at them."

Maria and I tiptoed downstairs. We tiptoed into the rec room. (I wondered why we were tiptoeing, if it was okay to look at the puppies.) We knelt by the pen, and I reached in to pat Astrid and her babies one more time.

"Who tied these ribbons?" I asked Maria. "They are in big knots. They look awful. Let's tie them in bows."

"Okay," said Maria. She and I each took the ribbon off of one puppy. A red ribbon and a green ribbon. Before we could tie them back on, though, Maria yelped, "My mom is coming!"

Maria and I flung ourselves behind a couch. But Mrs. Kilbourne walked right by the rec room.

"Phew! That was close!" exclaimed Maria. "Come on. Let's put the ribbons back on and get out of here." That was when Maria and I realized something. We did not know which ribbon to tie on which puppy. The puppies looked the same. So we just guessed. Then we ran out of the room.

Changes

The day after Maria and I had our puppy scare was a Thursday. Mommy and Andrew drove to school to pick Nancy and me up. When we returned home, I said to Nancy, "Want to play dolls?"

"Sure," replied Nancy. "I will go get my Barbies."

But Mommy said, "Can you girls wait half an hour? Karen, I want to talk to you and Andrew about something first."

"Oh, okay," I said. "Nancy, I will call you later."

Mommy and Andrew and I went inside. Mommy fixed us a snack and we sat around the kitchen table. I was beginning to feel nervous.

"Mommy? Is this bad news?" I asked.

"No," she replied. "But it is serious. Your father and I know that you two wish you could spend more time with Daddy."

"Equal time," spoke up Andrew. "That is fair. Like taking turns."

"You're right," said Mommy. "But we had made other arrangements. Also, I *like* spending lots of time with you. I love both of you very much. Anyway, because I love you, I want you to be happy. So Daddy and I have been talking to each other about this. And we have been talking to our lawyers. And guess what. I think we will be able to arrange for equal time. You two are very lucky. You are in a special situation. Daddy and I live very near to each other. Coming and going is easy for you. You do not have to change schools if we change the custody arrangements. And Daddy and I are on good terms. We talk to each other a lot. Not all divorced kids are so lucky. That is why I think switching to equal time will work out."

"Yes!" I cried. I jumped out of my chair. I raised my fist in the air.

"Yes! Yes! Yes!" cried Andrew. He jumped up, too.

"Now hold on," said Mommy. (But she was smiling.) "This is not definite yet. Before it can happen, a judge wants to talk to the two of you."

"A judge?" repeated Andrew. He frowned.

"Kind of like the principal at school," I told Andrew. "The person who is *really* in charge. Even in charge of the lawyers. The head person."

"Also a person who has a lot of experience making fair decisions," added Mommy.

"Why does the judge want to talk to us?" I asked.

"To make sure she makes the very best

decision possible. The judge knows what Daddy and I think, and she knows what our lawyers think. Now she wants to hear what you have to say. Then she will decide on the arrangements that will make everybody the happiest. She will just ask you some questions. All you have to do is answer them honestly. Tell her what you truly feel and what you truly want."

Our talk with the judge took place several days later. Andrew and I sat with her all by ourselves at a little table in a quiet room. Mommy and Daddy waited right outside. The judge was nice. She was young. She looked a little like my teacher, Ms. Colman. And she smiled a lot. She asked us questions about school and our friends and our two families.

"Easy questions!" Andrew said later. (No matter what I told him, he thought the judge was going to ask hard questions, like math problems.)

Not long after we talked with the judge,

Mommy and Daddy and Andrew and I went to a coffee shop together. Just the four of us. Just like when we used to be a family.

"Kids," began Mommy, "we have good news for you. Everyone has agreed on equal time. Even the judge. You are very lucky that the arrangements can be changed this easily." (Andrew started to jump up and shout. But I kicked his ankle. This was not the time for that.)

"This is what we have decided on," said Daddy. "Starting on the first day of next month, you will spend a month at the big house, then a month at the little house, and so on. Next year, we will switch the months so that you will not be at the same house each Thanksgiving or Christmas or for your birthdays."

"How does that sound?" asked Mommy.

"It sounds great," I replied. And it did — even though Mommy had begun to cry.

The Puppy Mix-up

I knew why Mommy was sad. It was because she would not see as much of Andrew and me. She would miss us. Andrew and I had asked for a big change. "But now," I said to Mommy one day, "I will see you just as much as I see Daddy. Even Steven. Fair is fair. Besides, when I am at Daddy's we can still talk on the phone. And if we have a program at school, you can still come to it. Plus, you will not have to get baby-sitters so often."

"Honey, I know," said Mommy. She

smiled. "I just need to get used to this idea. That's all. And you are right. Even Steven. Fair is fair."

I told myself to be extra nice to Mommy — Seth, too — and to remember to call her a lot when I was at Daddy's.

Meanwhile, another exciting thing was happening. The puppies were going to their new homes. They were old enough to leave Astrid. One day when Hannie and I went to Maria's house, only five puppies were left.

"And three more people are going to pick up their puppies today," said Maria.

"Oh, how can Astrid stand to see them go?" I asked. "That is so sad." For a moment, I thought of Mommy. She felt sad watching Andrew and me leave. And we were only leaving for a month. The puppies were leaving forever.

But Maria replied, "Astrid doesn't mind. Baby animals are supposed to leave their mothers." (I guess puppies are different from children.) "Come on! I hear a car. Let's see who is here."

A man and a boy came to the door. The boy was about my age. When Mr. Kilbourne let them inside, the boy ran to the puppies. "Hi, Bucko!" he cried. He picked up a puppy wearing a yellow ribbon. "You can finally come home with me! Wait until you see your bed!"

Just as Bucko was leaving with his new family, Mr. and Mrs. Franco arrived to pick up their puppy. " 'Bye, Bucko!" Maria and Hannie and I called. Then we followed the Francos to Astrid and her babies.

"Okay," said Mr. Kilbourne. "It's the red ribbon, isn't it?" He stooped down and picked up the puppy wearing the red ribbon. Then he handed it to Mrs. Franco. "Here you go."

Mrs. Franco reached for the puppy. But she did not take it. Instead, she leaned forward and stared at it.

"What is the matter?" asked her husband.

"This is not Twinkie," she replied. "This is not the puppy we chose."

"You're kidding," said Mr. Kilbourne.

"Dear, the Dodsons are here!" Mrs. Kilbourne called to Maria's father. And she led them inside.

Mr. Dodson reached for the puppy with the green ribbon. Then he drew back. "That is not Woody," he said.

"What is going on here?" asked Mr. Franco.

He sounded angry. Maria and I looked at each other. Uh-oh. The green ribbon and the red ribbon.

"Um," said Maria, "try switching the puppies."

Mrs. Franco picked up the Dodsons' puppy. Mr. Dodson picked up the Francos' puppy.

"Twinkie!" cried Mrs. Franco.

"Woody!" cried Mr. Dodson.

"Maria," said her father sharply. "How did you know the puppies had been switched?"

88

Maria and I had to tell our story then. The last thing Maria said was, "It was an accident. We are sorry."

"Really, really, really sorry," I added.

The Kilbournes were not *too* mad. (They just said they would talk to Maria later.) When Hannie and I left that day, we said good-bye to the rest of Astrid's puppies. The next time we visited, the puppies would be gone.

Bob

One morning I woke up at the little house and thought, "This is my last complete day here for one whole month." Andrew and I were going to the big house the next morning. For an entire, long month.

Guess what happened at breakfast. I had just put a spoonful of cereal in my mouth when Andrew said, "Excuse me! Excuse me! I have something to say. Excuse me, everybody!"

"Yes, Andrew?" said Seth.

"I have decided what pet to get."

Well, for heaven's sake. I had forgotten about Andrew and his pet.

"What did you decide on?" asked Mommy.

"A hermit crab. It is little, and it stays in a tank, and it is *very* easy to take care of."

"That sounds like a fine pet," said Mommy.

"Just fine," agreed Seth.

"We will go to the pet store this afternoon," added Mommy.

Andrew sang songs in the car on the way to the pet store. Mostly he sang "Bingo." "B-I-N-G-O! And Bingo was his name-o!"

"Bingo. That is a nice name. Is that what you are going to name your hermit crab?" I asked my brother.

"Nope," replied Andrew.

"Oh. What are you going to name it?"

"I don't know. I have to see whether it is a boy or a girl."

"Honey," said Mommy, "I am not sure

we will be able to tell a boy hermit crab from a girl hermit crab."

"The people at the pet store will," said Andrew.

And that was the end of that.

When we reached the pet store we walked straight to the counter.

"Let *me* talk!" Andrew whispered to Mommy.

"All right," she replied.

"Excuse me, sir," said Andrew to the man behind the counter. "Where are the hermit crabs?"

"Right over there," he said. He pointed to a tank.

Mommy and Andrew and I looked at the tank of tiny hermit crabs in their shells. Andrew looked the longest. He stood there forever. I felt bored. "Mom-*my*," I whined.

"Go look at the fish," Mommy said.

I think I stared at those fish for ten hours. When I returned to the hermit crabs, Andrew was still standing in front of the tank. He was saying, "Too little, ugly shell, bad colors, too shy," as he looked at each crab. But, finally, finally, finally he chose one.

The man behind the counter helped us find a tank and some other supplies. While he was ringing up our things, Andrew asked him, "Is my crab a boy or a girl?"

The man looked startled. "Uh, I'm not sure," he replied. "I can't tell."

I thought Andrew would be disappointed, but he just said, "*I* think it is a boy."

And *that* was the end of *that*.

"So," I said to Andrew as we were riding home in the car, "if your crab is a boy, what are you going to name him?"

Andrew glanced down at the tank in his lap. He squinched up his face. Then he said, "I am going to name him Bob."

A few minutes later, as we were pulling into our driveway, I realized something. Emily Junior and Bob were going to be two-twos with Andrew and me. So they would be Emily Two-two and Bob Two-two.

Good-bye and Hello

That night was the last night Andrew and I would spend at the little house for a long time. It was very busy.

First Mommy helped us get ready to switch houses. "You will not be back here for a month, so if you see something you cannot do without, bring it with you."

I knew what she meant. Since Andrew and I are two-twos, we have clothes and toys and stuff at both houses. But we do not have two of everything, and besides, *more* of our stuff is at Mommy's than at

Daddy's. I checked my school papers and my books and some art projects I was working on. I piled things into a box.

Then I had a talk with Emily Junior. "You are going to be a two-two from now on," I told her. "Just like me. Goldfishie and Crystal Light cannot be two-twos. They have to stay at the big house because it is not easy to move a fish tank full of water around. But you can go back and forth with me. And Bob can go back and forth with Andrew."

I packed up Emily's rat supplies. In the next room, Andrew was packing up his stuff, and Bob's crab supplies.

When we had finished packing, Mommy said, "Okay, time for dinner." That was all she said. So boy, were Andrew and I surprised when we walked into the dining room and found . . . a party! Mommy had put flowers on the table and tied balloons to the back of each chair. And Seth had fixed a special supper.

After dinner, we watched a video to-

gether. (Mommy had chosen *Mary Poppins*.) And we fixed popcorn. We pretended we were in a movie theater.

The next day was Tuesday. It was THE BIG DAY. I woke up early. I just could not sleep. Andrew could not sleep either. He tiptoed into my room in his pajamas. He climbed in bed with me.

"Karen?" he whispered. "What if we do not like staying at the big house for a month?"

"We will like it," I replied. "We love the big house. And we will not miss Daddy anymore."

"What if we miss Mommy?"

"Then we can call her. She will be right here with Seth." Andrew did not say anything. "Well, you know what?" I went on. "If we do not like these arrangements, we can always talk to Mommy and Daddy again. The judge will help us fix things. She wants us to be happy. Anyway, think of it, Andrew. The big house for a *month*! You can build all sorts of things with Sam. You can bake cookies with Nannie. Hey, we will get to see David Michael in his play! Best of all, Daddy will be there whenever we want him. And we will not have to go back and forth so often."

Andrew was smiling. "I can see Shannon," he added.

"And in a month, we will come back here."

After school that day, Mommy and Seth took Andrew and me to Daddy's. Mommy cried a little. So did Seth. So did Andrew and I.

"Good-bye!" I said, as Seth drove away.

"See you later, alligators!" Mommy called to us.

Andrew and I dried our tears as soon as we were inside the house. Daddy was there to greet us. He had come home from work early. He gave us big hugs.

Then Sam said, "Andrew, I have a new model airplane. Want to help me with it?"

And Kristy said, "Karen, come upstairs

with me. I will help you get Emily Junior settled. And tomorrow I want you to meet my friend Tess."

That was how our first month at the big house began. I thought it was off to a good start.

About the Author

ANN M. MARTIN lives in New York City and loves animals, especially cats. She has two cats of her own, Mouse and Rosie.

Other books by Ann M. Martin that you might enjoy are *Stage Fright*; *Me and Katie (the Pest)*; and the books in *The Baby-sitters Club* series.

Ann likes ice cream and *I Love Lucy*. And she has her own little sister, whose name is Jane.

Little Sister

Don't miss #49

KAREN'S STEPMOTHER

"Elizabeth is so mean," I said. "She is always telling me how to do things. She thinks her way is better. And she makes up too, too many rules. Do you know what? Everyone at the big house has to do chores. We have to do them *every day*. And if we don't, we do not get our allowance."

"I have to do chores, too," said Hannie.

"Well, I bet your mother does not tell you to be quiet all the time. Elizabeth says I talk too much, and I talk too loudly. And I interrupt."

Mrs. Papadakis pulled up in front of the school then. Hannie and I ran to our classroom to meet Nancy. The first thing I said to Nancy was, "Guess what. Elizabeth is awful. She makes up rules, and she is mean to me. Elizabeth is my wicked stepmother."

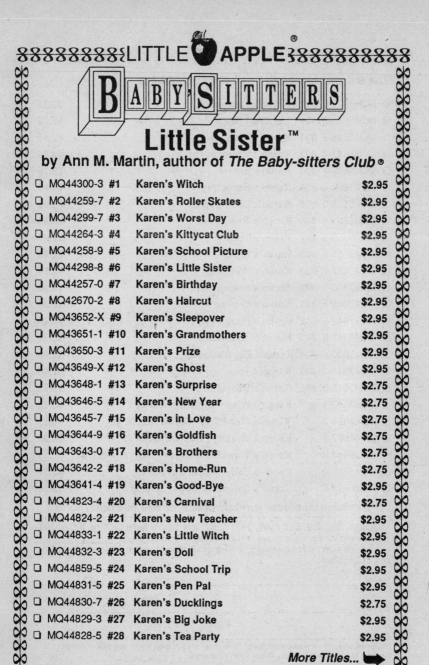

LITTLE APPLE ®

BABY·SITTERS

Little Sister ™

by Ann M. Martin, author of *The Baby-sitters Club* ®

❑ MQ44300-3	#1	Karen's Witch	$2.95
❑ MQ44259-7	#2	Karen's Roller Skates	$2.95
❑ MQ44299-7	#3	Karen's Worst Day	$2.95
❑ MQ44264-3	#4	Karen's Kittycat Club	$2.95
❑ MQ44258-9	#5	Karen's School Picture	$2.95
❑ MQ44298-8	#6	Karen's Little Sister	$2.95
❑ MQ44257-0	#7	Karen's Birthday	$2.95
❑ MQ42670-2	#8	Karen's Haircut	$2.95
❑ MQ43652-X	#9	Karen's Sleepover	$2.95
❑ MQ43651-1	#10	Karen's Grandmothers	$2.95
❑ MQ43650-3	#11	Karen's Prize	$2.95
❑ MQ43649-X	#12	Karen's Ghost	$2.95
❑ MQ43648-1	#13	Karen's Surprise	$2.75
❑ MQ43646-5	#14	Karen's New Year	$2.75
❑ MQ43645-7	#15	Karen's in Love	$2.75
❑ MQ43644-9	#16	Karen's Goldfish	$2.75
❑ MQ43643-0	#17	Karen's Brothers	$2.75
❑ MQ43642-2	#18	Karen's Home-Run	$2.75
❑ MQ43641-4	#19	Karen's Good-Bye	$2.95
❑ MQ44823-4	#20	Karen's Carnival	$2.75
❑ MQ44824-2	#21	Karen's New Teacher	$2.95
❑ MQ44833-1	#22	Karen's Little Witch	$2.95
❑ MQ44832-3	#23	Karen's Doll	$2.95
❑ MQ44859-5	#24	Karen's School Trip	$2.95
❑ MQ44831-5	#25	Karen's Pen Pal	$2.95
❑ MQ44830-7	#26	Karen's Ducklings	$2.75
❑ MQ44829-3	#27	Karen's Big Joke	$2.95
❑ MQ44828-5	#28	Karen's Tea Party	$2.95

More Titles... ➡

Available wherever you buy books, or use this order form.

Scholastic Inc., P.O. Box 7502, 2931 E. McCarty Street, Jefferson City, MO 65102

Please send me the books I have checked above. I am enclosing $ _____
(please add $2.00 to cover shipping and handling). Send check or money order - no cash
or C.O.Ds please.

Name _____ Birthdate_____

Address _____

City _____ State/Zip_____

Please allow four to six weeks for delivery. Offer good in U.S.A. only. Sorry, mail orders are not
available to residents to Canada. Prices subject to change.   BLS793